TIME-OUT FOR
SOPHIE

ROSEMARY WELLS

VIKING
An Imprint of Penguin Group (USA) Inc.

Sophie's mama made Sophie a beautiful supper.

"Yum yum!" said Sophie.
"Good Sophie!" said Sophie's mama.

Then Sophie threw her supper on the floor.
"No, Sophie," said Mama. "No throwing supper!"

Mama tried again.

"Cookie!" said Sophie

"Time-out for Sophie!" said Mama.

So Sophie had a time-out.

It was Daddy's turn to fold the laundry.
"Helping!" said Sophie.

"Good Sophie!" said Daddy.
Daddy hung the socks on the line.

But when Daddy wasn't looking, Sophie pushed
the whole pile of folded laundry onto the floor.

"Daddy folding laundry again!" said Sophie.
"No pushing over the laundry, Sophie!" said Daddy.

But . . .

Sophie pushed all the laundry onto the floor again.

"Time-out for Sophie!" said Sophie's daddy.

So Sophie had another time-out.

"Read a book!" said Sophie.
"Please!" said Sophie's granny.
"Please!" said Sophie.
Granny read Sophie a story.

But Sophie grabbed Granny's glasses off her nose.

"No grabbing glasses, Sophie," said Granny.

Sophie did it again

and again.

"Time-out for Granny," said Granny.

"No time-out, Granny! No time-out!"

Sophie put Granny's glasses back on Granny's nose.

There was no throwing. There was no pushing.
There was no grabbing.
"Good Sophie!" said Granny.

"Good Sophie!" said Sophie.

For Petra Schuyler Wells

VIKING
Published by the Penguin Group
Penguin Young Readers Group, 345 Hudson Street, New York, New York 10014, U.S.A.
Penguin Group (Canada), 90 Eglinton Avenue East, Suite 700, Toronto, Ontario, Canada M4P 2Y3
(a division of Pearson Penguin Canada Inc.)
Penguin Books Ltd, 80 Strand, London WC2R 0RL, England
Penguin Ireland, 25 St Stephen's Green, Dublin 2, Ireland (a division of Penguin Books Ltd)
Penguin Group (Australia), 250 Camberwell Road, Camberwell, Victoria 3124, Australia
(a division of Pearson Australia Group Pty Ltd)
Penguin Books India Pvt Ltd, 11 Community Centre, Panchsheel Park, New Delhi – 110 017, India
Penguin Group (NZ), 67 Apollo Drive, Rosedale, Auckland 0632, New Zealand
(a division of Pearson New Zealand Ltd.)
Penguin Books (South Africa) (Pty) Ltd, 24 Sturdee Avenue, Rosebank, Johannesburg 2196, South Africa

Penguin Books Ltd, Registered Offices: 80 Strand, London WC2R 0RL, England

First published in the United States of America by Viking, a division of Penguin Young Readers Group, 2013

1 3 5 7 9 10 8 6 4 2

Copyright © Rosemary Wells, 2013
All rights reserved

LIBRARY OF CONGRESS CATALOGING-PUBLICATION-DATA
Wells, Rosemary.
Time-out for Sophie / by Rosemary Wells.
p. cm.
Summary: Although Sophie wants to be helpful and good, sometimes she ignores her mother, father,
and grandmother and must have a time-out.
ISBN 978-0-670-78511-7 (hardcover)
[1. Behavior—Fiction. 2. Family life—Fiction.] I. Title.
PZ7.W46843Tho 2013
[E]—dc23
2012015263

Manufactured in China   Set in Kennerley
The art for this book was created using ink, watercolor, gouache, and fabric.

Thanks to Windham Fabrics, Maywood Studio Fabrics, RJR Fabrics, Moda Fabrics, Darlene Zimmerman,
Judy Rothermel, Kaye England, and Barbara Brackman for the use of the fabrics in this book.

ALWAYS LEARNING   PEARSON